Minerva Louise
on Halloween

Janet Morgan Stoeke

Dutton Children's Books

For Chester L. Brooks

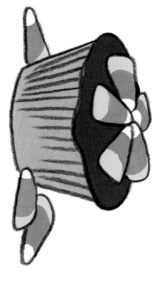

DUTTON CHILDREN'S BOOKS
A division of Penguin Young Readers Group

Published by the Penguin Group
Penguin Group (USA) Inc., 375 Hudson Street, New York, New York 10014, U.S.A. • Penguin Group (Canada), 90 Eglinton Avenue East, Suite 700, Toronto,
Ontario M4P 2Y3, Canada (a division of Pearson Penguin Canada Inc.) • Penguin Books Ltd, 80 Strand, London WC2R 0RL, England • Penguin Ireland, 25 St
Stephen's Green, Dublin 2, Ireland (a division of Penguin Books Ltd) • Penguin Group (Australia), 250 Camberwell Road, Camberwell, Victoria 3124, Australia
(a division of Pearson Australia Group Pty Ltd) • Penguin Books India Pvt Ltd, 11 Community Centre, Panchsheel Park, New Delhi—110 017, India • Penguin
Group (NZ), 67 Apollo Drive, Rosedale, North Shore 0632, New Zealand (a division of Pearson New Zealand Ltd) • Penguin Books (South Africa) (Pty) Ltd,
24 Sturdee Avenue, Rosebank, Johannesburg 2196, South Africa • Penguin Books Ltd, Registered Offices: 80 Strand, London WC2R 0RL, England

Library of Congress Cataloging-in-Publication Data
Stoeke, Janet Morgan.
Minerva Louise on Halloween / Janet Morgan Stoeke.—1st ed.   p. cm.
Summary: On her first Halloween, Minerva Louise the hen puzzles over
costumes but enjoys her first taste of candy corn.
ISBN 978-0-525-42149-8
[1. Chickens—Fiction. 2. Halloween—Fiction.] 1. Title.
PZ7.S8696Mlp 2009   [E]—dc22   2008034218

Published in the United States by Dutton Children's Books,
a division of Penguin Young Readers Group
345 Hudson Street, New York, New York 10014
www.penguin.com/youngreaders

Designed by Abby Kuperstock
Manufactured in China • First Edition
1 3 5 7 9 10 8 6 4 2

Minerva Louise loved it in the fall
when the pumpkins came for a visit.

She'd sit with them and watch the farmers, who never stopped working, even for a minute.

It was one of her favorite things to do.

But she wasn't sure if the pumpkins enjoyed it as much as she did.

This will be fun, she said. The farmers are planting a garden. A rock garden!

Everyone is helping. These two are bringing over a hoe and a rake.

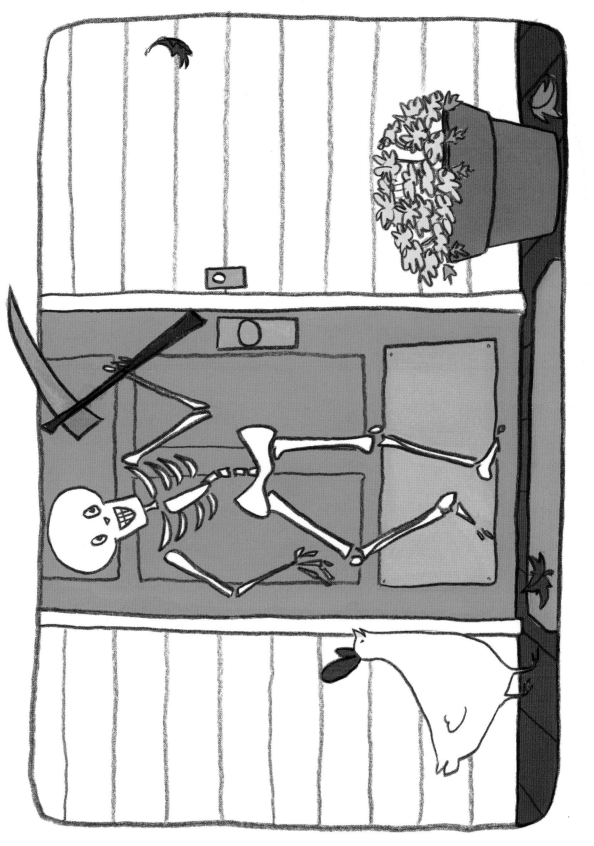

Here's a farmer with a shovel,
but he looks too skinny to dig.

And this one has some flowers to plant
and a watering can!

They've all been working so hard. Look, they're drinking to the bottom of their water bucket!

Oh, hello! Did you put up the new curtains? I just love the blackbirds on them.

Oh, my. What happened here?
What's gotten you guys so fired up?

Oh, that? Don't worry. That's just the laundry.

Although laundry usually stays on the clothesline, doesn't it?

Wait, it's not laundry. It's farmers! And they're bringing feed buckets to the door.

Look! They're getting corn! I love corn!
Where's my feed bucket?

Now if I can just . . .

Aha! I got it! Ding-dong!

Trick or treat!

Wow, CORN! This is great!!

And it's the sweetest corn ever! Try some!

Did you hear that lady farmer? She said I had such a clever costume.

But I'm not even wearing one!